$\mathcal{A}$
atheneum

ATHENEUM BOOKS FOR YOUNG READERS
An imprint of Simon & Schuster Children's Publishing Division
1230 Avenue of the Americas, New York, New York 10020

ATHENEUM BOOKS FOR YOUNG READERS is a registered trademark of
Simon & Schuster, Inc.
Atheneum logo is a trademark of Simon & Schuster, Inc.
For information about special discounts for bulk purchases, please
contact Simon & Schuster Special Sales at 1-866-506-1949 or
business@simonandschuster.com.
The Simon & Schuster Speakers Bureau can bring authors to your
live event. For more information or to book an event, contact the
Simon & Schuster Speakers Bureau at 1-866-248-3049 or visit our
website at www.simonspeakers.com.
Book design by Ann Bobco
The text for this book is set in Big Caslon.
The illustrations for this book are rendered in
watercolor and colored pencil.
Manufactured in China
0315 SCP
First Edition
2 4 6 8 10 9 7 5 3 1
Library of Congress Cataloging-in-Publication Data
Averbeck, Jim.
One word from Sophia / Jim Averbeck ; illustrated by Yasmeen
Ismail.
pages cm
Summary: All Sophie wants for her birthday is a pet giraffe, but as
she tries to convince different members of her rather complicated
family to support her cause, each tells her she is using too many
words until she finally hits on the perfect one. Includes glossary.
ISBN 978-1-4814-0514-0 (hardcover)
ISBN 978-1-4814-0515-7 (eBook)
[1. Interpersonal communication—Fiction.
2. Family life—Fiction. 3. Giraffe—Fiction.
4. Birthdays—Fiction. 5. Humorous stories.]
I. Ismail, Yasmeen, illustrator. II. Title.
PZ7.A933816One 2015
[E]—dc23
2014024661

For the Averbeck family—J. A.

For Ania—Y. I.

jim averbeck and yasmeen ismail

One Word

from

Sophia

One word for you – READ!
'15

Atheneum Books for Young Readers

New York London Toronto Sydney New Delhi

Sophia's birthday was coming up, and she had five things on her mind—
One True Desire and four problems.

Her One True Desire was to get a pet giraffe for her birthday.

The four problems were . . .

Mother,
who was a judge,

Father,
who was a businessman,

Uncle Conrad,
who was a politician,

and Grand-mamá,
who was very strict.

Sophia presented her case to Mother.

"I would like a giraffe," she said, "because they burn less gasoline, so they meet federal regulations better than the cars we use now. In the last fifty years, no giraffes have been recalled for defective parts, and newer models have a particularly strong safety record. Also, giraffes have not been shown to be the cause of any major diseases. Giraffes are legal in all fifty states.

"And a giraffe could take me to ballet class and deliver me right to the second floor."

Her argument was accompanied by a compelling slideshow that included a map of the walk to class.

"I'm sorry," said Mother in her decision, "but I will have to rule against a giraffe at this time. You provided no proof that you are ready for pet ownership and failed to cite any laws about minors driving quadrupeds.

"And your argument was too verbose."

"Verbose?" asked Sophia. "What's that mean?"

"Too many words," said Mother.

"How many should I use?"

"Fewer," said Mother, and she retired to her chambers.

So Sophia used fewer words with Father.

"Giraffes," said Sophia, "are a good source of manure, which can be sold at a profit to garden centers and activists.

"In short, people will pay me for poop."

Sophia polled the other members of the household . . .

. . . and presented the results to Uncle Conrad.

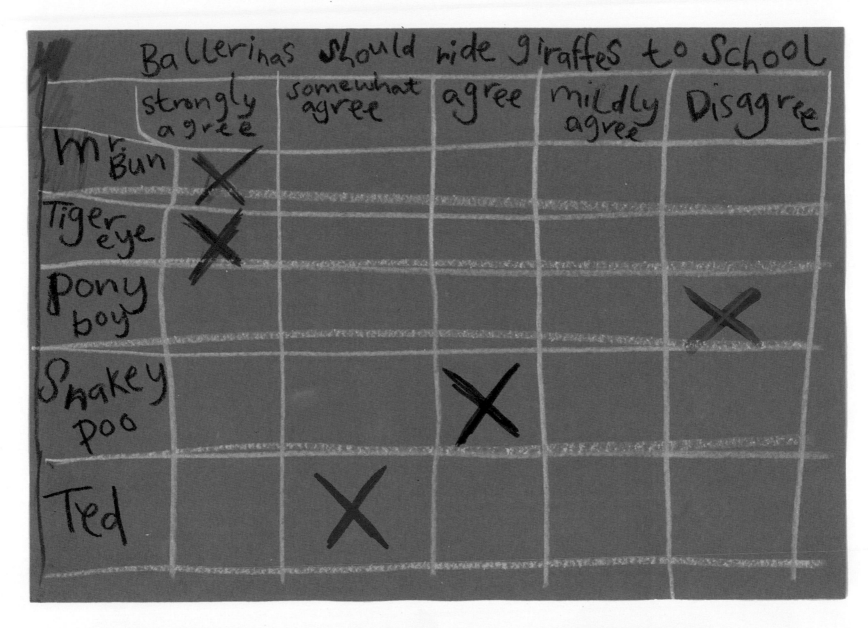

"Four out of five respondents are in favor of giraffes," she said.

The results were
accompanied
by a compelling
pie chart.

"I'm sorry," said Uncle Conrad, "but your results indicate that being in favor of giraffe ownership would cost me support from the Pony-American community. And besides, your report was far too loquacious."

Sophia didn't even need to ask.

Finally she approached Grand-mamá.

She accompanied her plea with a compelling foot rub.

"Giraf—"

"**No**," said Grand-mamá,
"and *do* try to get to the point next time."

In a last, desperate attempt before her birthday, Sophia prepared to speak to everyone at once. She revised and shortened her proposition until it was just one word:

Please.

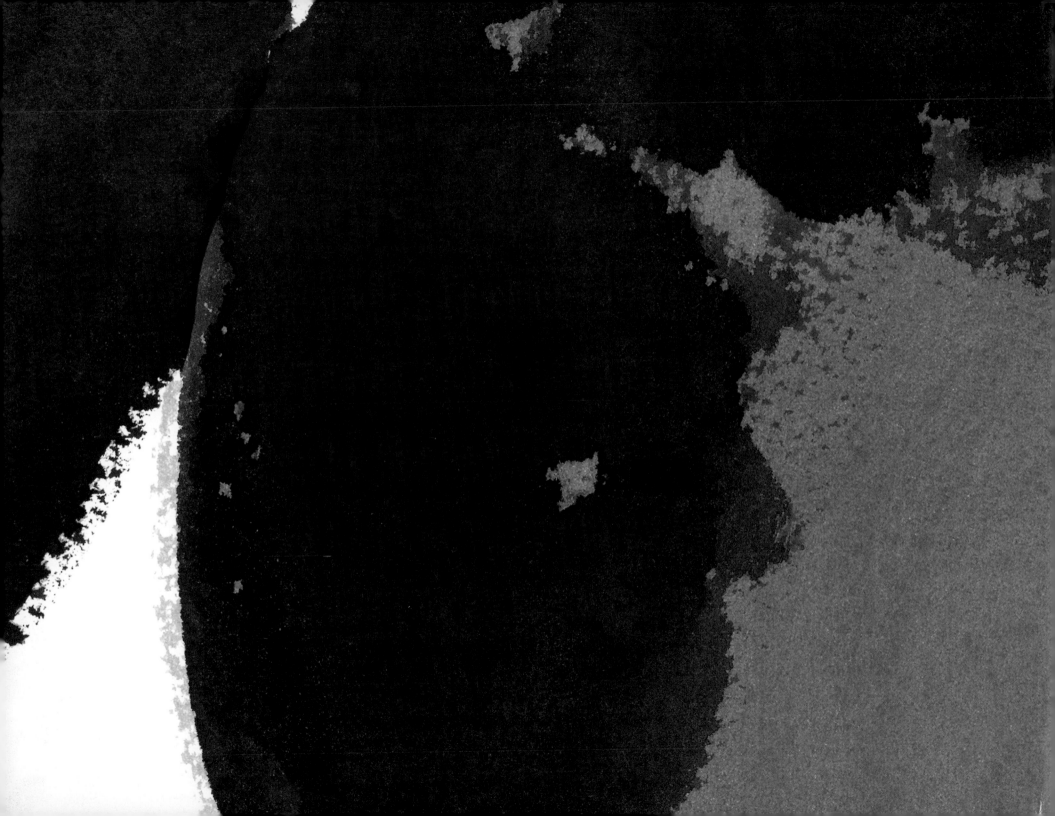

The proposal was
accompanied by a
particularly compelling
pair of eyes.

On her birthday, Sophia was delighted to find that short and sweet often brings results.

"One word really worked," she said.

And two words came in handy as well:

Thank
You.